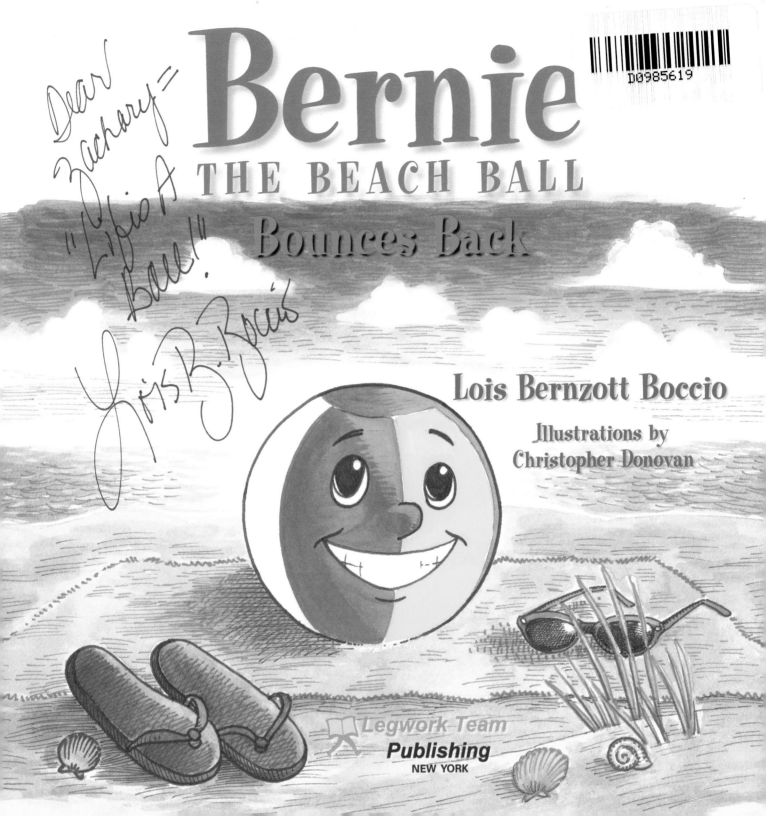

Bernie
THE BEACH BALL
Bounces Back

Lois Bernzott Boccio

Illustrations by
Christopher Donovan

*Dear Zachary —
"Lift off Ball!"*
Lois B. Boccio

D0985619

Legwork Team
Publishing
NEW YORK

Legwork Team
Publishing

Legwork Team Publishing
80 Davids Drive, Suite One
Hauppauge, NY 11788
www.legworkteam.com
Phone: 631-944-6511

ISBN: 978-0-9827337-8-3(sc)

First edition 09/01/2010

Printed in the United States of America
This book is printed on acid-free paper

Illustrations by Christopher Donovan
Designed by Vaiva Ulenas-Boertje

To my first family:
Mom, Dad and Lisa
and to my own family:
Andrew, Melanie and Brittany
... you ALL have inspired me to be
a better mom and person.

"I wonder if today will be the day," said Bernie. "I've been hanging here all winter waiting for the first day of summer vacation. Why doesn't anyone pick me? Maybe because I'm the smallest one left and ... I'm on sale! Summer discount rack! How humiliating!"

"Oh wait a minute, here comes someone now. Okay, stay straight, look colorful, act bouncy, oh … oh … wow … he's raising his hand, he's coming to me … aaaaaand … YES HE PICKED ME! THAT'S IT … I'm free, I'm outta here!"

Mel was about to enjoy the first day of summer vacation at the beach with his dad.

Mel's dad didn't live with him or his mom anymore so he just saw him on weekends. He always looked forward to seeing his dad and couldn't wait to see what adventure his father had planned for them. His dad didn't have much money to treat him to video games, new sneakers or the skateboard he'd been wanting, but it didn't matter to Mel. Being with his dad was all that mattered to him.

"I sure do love this kid for picking me and it looks like he's packing for some trip. The cooler's packed with drinks and snacks, the car is running; hope the air conditioning is on. But what about me? What's this, oh man … a beach umbrella … that's it? This is MY moment! I can't be left behind in the garage with this dented Frisbee and a hoola-hoop that probably nobody's used since…. Ah! I knew it, he sees me; he's coming, he's coming right for me and YES IT's ME … HE LIKES ME … HE REALLY LIKES ME! I'm on my way! See ya 'Freaky Frisbee;' better luck mañana!"

"Oh, what a glorious day; the sun is shining, the water
is perfect and oh, wow, look at the curves on that beach ball.
Hey baby ... that's right, how you doin'?"

"Ahhh this is it ... the exact moment a beach ball like me waits for his whole life. I guess I could use the rest and stretch myself a little; that drive over here was just dreadful, putting me in the trunk, the TRUNK! What am I an old tire?"

"Wow it sure is getting windy. The sand is really flying up and look at those waves! Oh here comes a big gust now ... Oh noooo, oh noooo. HEEEEEEEELP!"

Caught by the wind, Bernie flies high above the people on the beach, spiraling down and landing on the blanket of a Grandma with her granddaughter who quickly snatches him up.

"Oh my, look what just landed on us!" said Brittany as she smiled. "I wonder where it came from?"

She looks around the beach but doesn't see anyone who looks like they lost it.

"Oh well, guess you're mine now," she said.

Mel returning from a walk with his dad noticed that the ball was gone.

"Dad, did you see the ball? It was just here a minute ago."

"No, I didn't son," he answered while taking a soda out of the cooler.

"Oh man … I liked that ball!"

"Oh great, just great. I mean this little girl looks okay *although the Grandma looks like she's been in the sun too long* ... but I want my boy back! Hey Mel, I'm over here ... OH I WISH I HAD A HAND TO WAVE WITH!"

Brittany noticed a boy going from blanket to blanket asking questions and thought HE might be the owner of the ball. She picked up the ball and carried it over to him.

"Is this what you're looking for?" she asked.

He looked down at her and realized that she too, liked the ball.

"Hey, thanks. It must have blown away when I went for a walk with my dad. We're just sitting over there where the big white cooler is. Listen, if you really like it you can have it."

"Really, are you sure, because I don't want to take it if you really want it?"
"No, that's okay, the summer's just starting ... I'll get another one."

"Another one! Another one! What am I, an old toothbrush? He can't get rid of me just like that! I thought I meant something to him! Although, wait a minute. He's walking away and he doesn't look too happy even though he's smiling. That's right Mel, smile through the pain!"

Mel and his dad decided to go up to the snack bar to get some ice cream. When they were returning, they saw that the sky was changing to a cloudy gray and they knew the rain the weatherman predicted was probably on its way. Suddenly, the sky opened up and the rain began to pelt Mel and his dad as they ran for the car.

All the way home the rain fell hard and came down in buckets. They laughed together realizing how lucky their timing had been, leaving the beach when they did. Once they got back to the garage they began to unpack the cooler and shake the sand off their feet. Mel opened the cooler to get a soda. There to his amazement, sitting inside the cooler was …

Bernie!

Brittany realized that Mel really did want his beach ball and was just being nice when he gave it to her. So when Mel and his dad went to the snack bar, she walked over to his blanket and snuck it into his cooler.

"Bye beach ball," she whispered and closed the lid.

"Wow, it really does pay to be nice," said Mel.

"I'm baaaaack!" said Bernie.

ABOUT THE AUTHOR

Lois Bernzott Boccio has had careers in advertising, private investigation and Off-Broadway Theater, but her passion has always been writing, especially children's books. She feels that a child's favorite book is like "having your own special friend." She lives on the East End of Long Island with her husband, two daughters, and her beloved Lab, Shelby. She got her inspiration for *Bernie the Beach Ball Bounces Back* while "people-watching" during summer vacations on the beautiful beaches of Montauk and the Hamptons with her family and friends.

Turn the page
for your
FREE
Beach Ball!

For more information regarding Lois Bernzott Boccio and her work,
visit her web site: www.LoisBernzottBoccio.com.

Additional copies of this book may be purchased online from
LegworkTeam.com; Amazon.com;
or via the author's web site: www.LoisBernzottBoccio.com.

You can also obtain a copy of the book by visiting
L.I. Books Bookstore
80 Davids Drive, Suite One
Hauppauge, NY 11788
or ordering it from your favorite bookstore.

LaVergne, TN USA
17 September 2010
197556LV00001B